Dooby Dooby moo

by
doreen cronin
and
betsy lewin

SIMON AND SCHUSTER

Farmer Brown keeps a very close eye on his animals. Every night he listens outside the barn door.

Dooby, dooby moo . . .
the cows snore.

Fa la, la, la baaaa . . .
the sheep snore.

Whacka, whacka quack . . .
Duck snores.

For Mom
— D. C.

To Claire Rose Reilly
and Logan Patrick McMurray
— B. L.

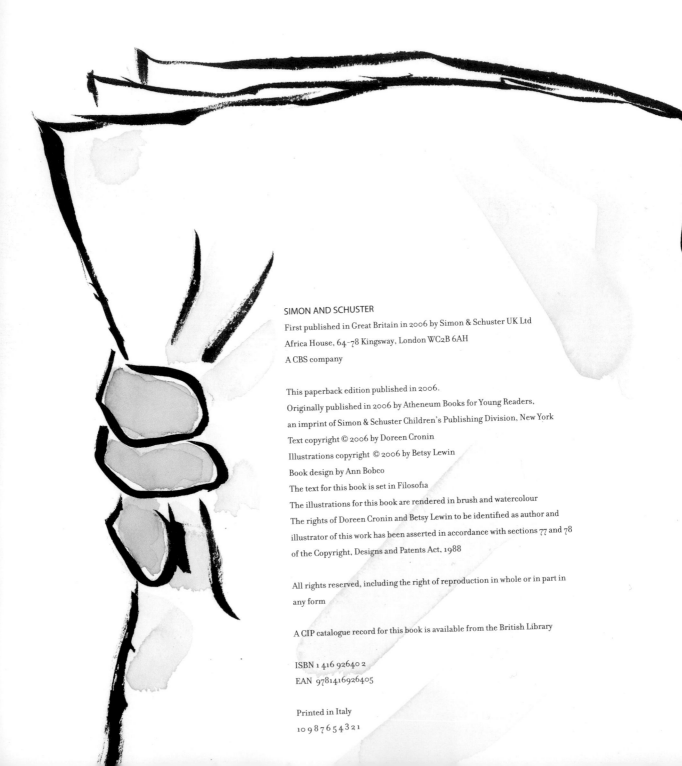

SIMON AND SCHUSTER

First published in Great Britain in 2006 by Simon & Schuster UK Ltd

Africa House, 64–78 Kingsway, London WC2B 6AH

A CBS company

This paperback edition published in 2006.

Originally published in 2006 by Atheneum Books for Young Readers,

an imprint of Simon & Schuster Children's Publishing Division, New York

Text copyright © 2006 by Doreen Cronin

Illustrations copyright © 2006 by Betsy Lewin

Book design by Ann Bobco

The text for this book is set in Filosofia

The illustrations for this book are rendered in brush and watercolour

The rights of Doreen Cronin and Betsy Lewin to be identified as author and

illustrator of this work has been asserted in accordance with sections 77 and 78

of the Copyright, Designs and Patents Act, 1988

A CIP catalogue record for this book is available from the British Library

ISBN 1 416 92640 2

EAN 9781416926405

Printed in Italy

10 9 8 7 6 5 4 3 2 1

Duck keeps a very close eye
on Farmer Brown.

Every morning Duck borrows
his newspaper. One day,
an ad catches his eye:

TALENT SHOW!!!

OPEN TO ALL!!

where: COUNTY FAIR
when: SATURDAY

1st prize: A TRAMPOLINE!!*

2nd prize: BOX OF CHALK**

3rd prize: VEGGIE CHOP-O-MATIC

* Slightly used. Sponsor makes no warranty, expressed or implied, nor assumes any responsibility in the use of the trampoline. Actual amount awarded will be based on availability.

** Actual amount awarded will be based on availability.

As soon as Farmer Brown opened his paper, he knew the animals were up to something.

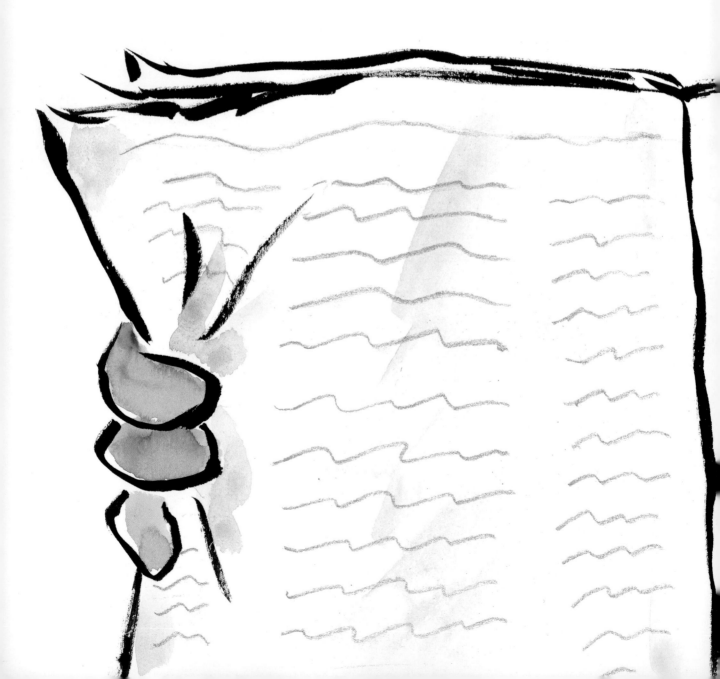

Farmer Brown watched them closely all day.

He watched them
from above.

He watched them from below.

He even watched them upside down.

Outside the barn, late at night, he heard,

Dooby, dooby moo . . .
Fa la, la, la baaaa . . .
Whacka, whacka QUack . . .

Inside the barn, the cows rehearsed "Twinkle, Twinkle, Little Star."

Dooby, dooby, dooby moo.
Dooby moo, moo, moo, moo, moo.

Needs work, Duck noted.

The sheep rehearsed
"Home on the Range."

Baaa, baaa, baaa, baaabaaa.
Fa la baaa, fa la baaaa, baaaabaaabaaa!

Duck had them try it again,
with more feeling.

The pigs did an interpretive dance.

whacka, whacka
QUaaack . . .

snored Duck.

Day after day, Farmer Brown kept a very close eye on the animals.

He watched from the left.

He watched from the right.

He even watched in disguise.

Outside the barn, night after night, he heard:

Dooby, dooby moo . . .

Fa la, la, la baaaa . . .

Whacka, whacka quack . . .

Inside the barn, night after night, the animals rehearsed.

Finally it was time for the county fair.

Duck was
pacing
back
and forth.

The pigs were combing their hair.

The cows were drinking tea with lemon.

They ARE up to something!
thought Farmer Brown.

Farmer Brown
was not going
to leave them alone.

He loaded all the animals into the

back of his truck and drove to the fair.

When he got there he heard:

Dooby, dooby moo . . .

Fa la, la, la baaaa . . .

Whacka, whacka quack . . .

He parked his truck and headed off to
the free barbecue.

When Farmer Brown was out of sight,
the animals ran to the talent show desk
and signed in.*

Cows
Sheep
Pigs

The cows sang
"Twinkle, Twinkle, Little Star."

Dooby, dooby, dooby moo.

Dooby moo, moo, moo, moo, moo.

Two of the judges were clearly impressed.

The sheep sang "Home on the Range."

la, la baa.

ba, ba, baaa, baa, ba, baaaa.

Three of the judges were clearly impressed.

It was time for the pigs' interpretive dance.
But they were sound asleep.

Shloink oink, oink, oink, oink.

All of the judges were clearly annoyed.

Duck really wanted that trampoline.
He jumped on stage and sang
"Born to Be Wild."*

QUack, QUack, QUuuaaaaaaCKK!

The judges gave him a standing ovation.

*Original words and music by Mars Bonfire

When Farmer Brown got back to the truck, he heard:

Dooby, dooby moo . . .
Fa la, la, la baaaa . . .
Whacka, whacka Quack . . .

The animals were exactly where he had left them.

That night Farmer Brown listened outside the barn door.

Dooby, dooby BOING!

Fa la, la, la BOING!

Whacka, whacka BOING!